Marlon Bundo's
Best Christmas Ever

Written by CHARLOTTE PENCE

Illustrated by KAREN PENCE

Regnery Kids

Regnery Kids™ is a trademark of Salem Communications Holding Corporation;
Regnery® is a registered trademark of Salem Communications Holding Corporation

Cataloging-in-Publication data on file with the Library of Congress

ISBN: 978-1-62157-870-3
e-book ISBN: 978-1-62157-871-0

Published in the United States by
Regnery Kids, an imprint of
Regnery Publishing
A Division of Salem Media Group
300 New Jersey Ave NW
Washington, DC 20001
www.RegneryKids.com

Published in association with the literary agency of Wolgemuth & Associates, Inc.

Manufactured in the United States of America

10 9 8 7 6 5 4 3 2 1

Books are available in quantity for promotional or premium use. For information on discounts and
terms, please visit our website: www.Regnery.com

This book is dedicated to our loving family and
all the magical moments we share.

Dad

Michael and Sarah

Audrey and Dan

Henry

If you haven't met me before,
my name is Marlon Bundo Pence.
I live with my grandparents at
the vice president's residence.

My Grampa is the vice president
and my Grandma is the second lady.
They're here to serve the United States,
but to me they're just family.

6

It's getting close to the holidays
and the snow is starting to fall.
In the next room over, I can hear
Grandma on an important call.

She's planning the holiday party
with carols and lots of guests.
Staff members bring along their loved ones
and we all feel very blessed!

The party is in a few hours.
Preparations are fast underway!
It will be a festive occasion—
volunteers have been working all day.

I, too, want to help my Grandma,
but I don't have a single clue.
I scurry over to Grampa
and ask, "What's a bunny to do?"

The VP leans down very close
and whispers in my furry ear,
"What Grandma loves the most of all
is bringing people lots of cheer."

True, I am just a bunny,
and sometimes I feel so small.
But I can help in one way:
create one giant gift for all!

On the main floor of the big house,
decorations are everywhere.
I ask a local nutcracker
if he has something small to share.

As I hop along the corridors
of this special historic house,
I pass some of the Secret Service.
I hope they know I'm not a mouse!

I ask one agent politely,
"May I please borrow a 'hard pin'?"
He leans down and hands one to me,
not touching my ticklish chin.

Nearby, tuning her instrument,
is a member of the band.
I hop on over to see her
and stand up to nudge her hand.

She's one of the Navy sailors,
and I explain what I want to make.
She nods her head, then smiles and says,
"Here is something fun that you can
take."

She plucks off a bit of holly
decorating the musical stand.
I thank her and carry it off,
the busiest bunny in the land!

15

Next, I go to the menorah
to find something my ornament lacks.
I scurry onto the table
to nibble off some blue candle wax.

The menorah is a very special part
of a history so great.
We light a candle each night of Hanukah
and in total there are eight!

Over there away in a manger,
with small figures just my size,
I borrow a gift from the Magi
and they still look just as wise!

I spy some wrapping paper
that has fallen to the ground.
I snatch it and sneak away,
careful not to make a sound!

Shiny stars hang in the stairway—
they look so merry and divine.
Glitter flutters onto the ground—
that will be great for added shine!

I grab gold string that is hanging,
to keep them dangling above.
I will use it for my gift, too,
and I think I'll have enough!

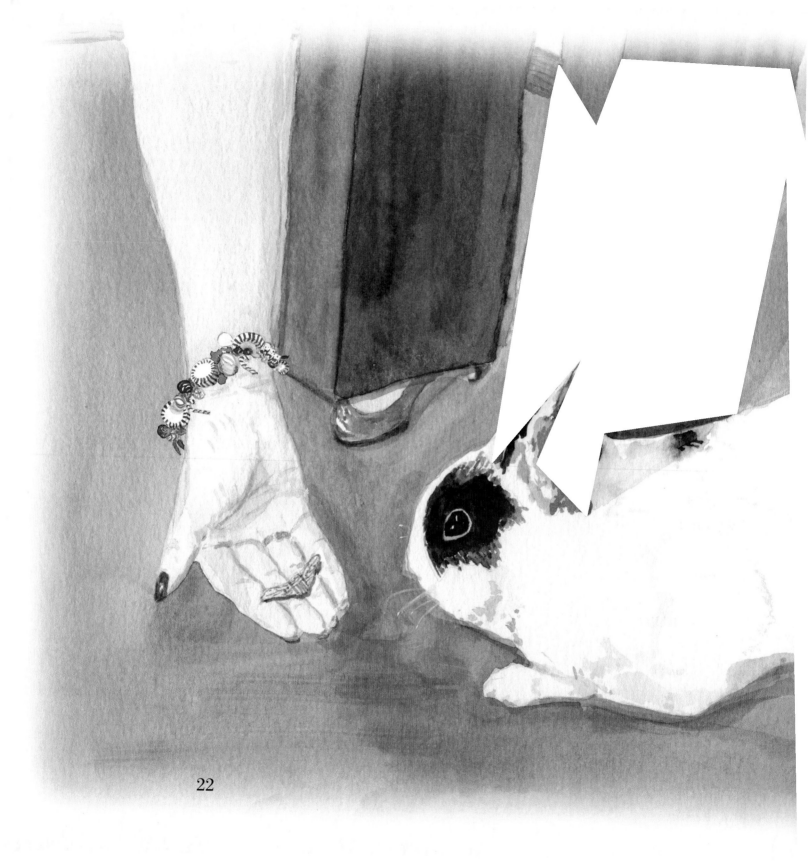

But wait, some staff are arriving.
They're the pilots from Air Force Two.
I ask them to borrow their wings.
It is perfect! They look brand new!

A small girl runs up to greet me,
and hands me a sparkly thing.
A word stitched on a red ribbon—
"Joy!"—It has a holiday ring!

Now I have each part from our home
to complete the big celebration.
With a snip, snap, wrap, and a tap,
I hurry to make my creation.

Finally, I need something sticky
to hold all the parts in one piece.
In the kitchen, I find what I need:
honey from our own hive of bees!

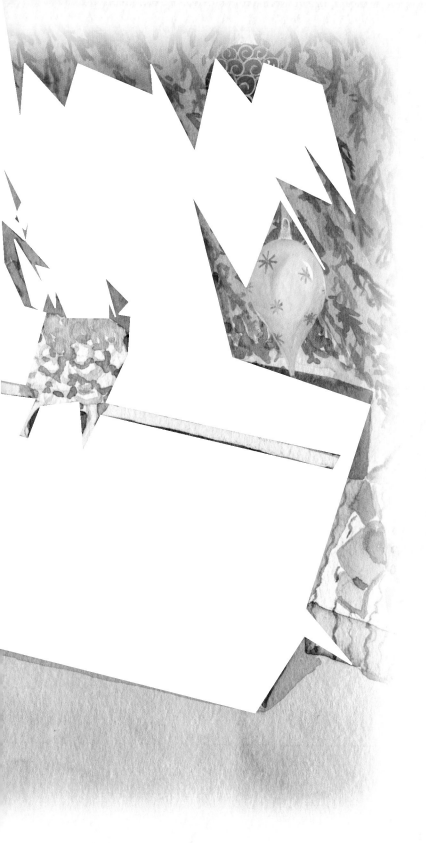

From many customs, faiths, and people,
and all different colors, sizes, and shapes,
each piece makes up a unique story
just like our country—the United States!

I put it all together
and inspect it up and down.
It is so big and messy,
but also perfect somehow.

I twitch my cute nose to scoot
the ornament under the tree.
I sure hope Grandma finds it,
and it makes her very happy!

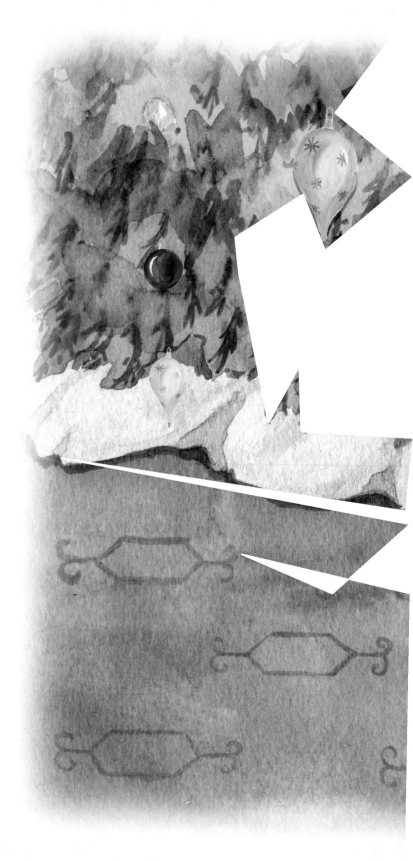

I see the big clock on the wall—
it's already 8:05!
It's time to scurry up the stairs
to watch as the guests arrive.

I feel so blessed to be here
looking down at the people below.
They gather close together
in the holiday spirit we know.

From here I can clearly see
it is laughter, love, and joy
that bring us all together—
not just gifts and fancy toys.

35

And when I made my ornament,
I could not have done it alone.
I needed help from my dear friends,
and all the kindness they have shown!

So this is the miracle of Christmas:
each of us has our own gift to bring,
even if it is just one ornament,
held together with honey and string.

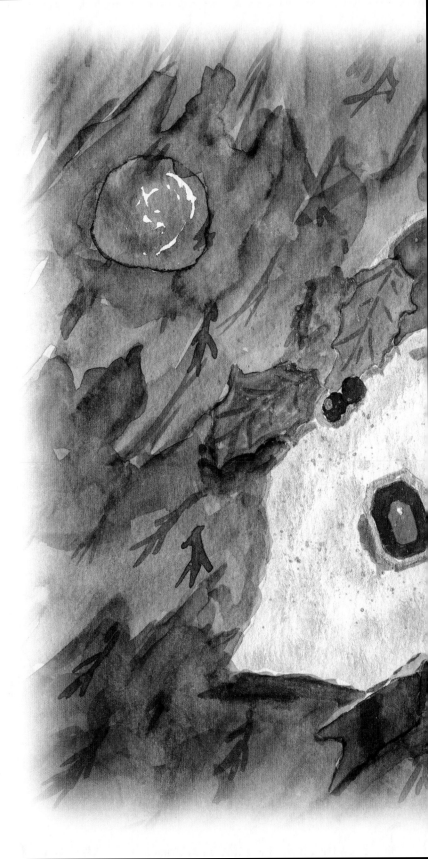

A Christmas Message

From

The Pences

The holiday season is a magical time when people all over the world gather together with their loved ones. It's a special time of year when we are able to take a moment to appreciate the people who love and support us year-round.

Marlon learns that what makes this time of year so special are not the gifts that we receive, but rather the people with whom we share our most cherished memories.

In our house, we celebrate Christmas at this time of year. This is a sacred time when we remember God's gift to the world, and we celebrate the birth of Jesus.

May your holiday season be filled with special moments with those *you* love.

And may you always remember to look for the magic all year long.